Monty Goes to the fish ZOO

by Vivienne Alonge

Illustrated by Mikaila Maidment

Monty the Fish Goes to the Zoo

Vivienne Alonge

Published by 1st World Publishing
P.O. Box 2211, Fairfield, Iowa 52556
tel: 641-209-5000 • fax: 866-440-5234
web: www.1stworldpublishing.com

First Edition

LCCN: 2014909870
SoftCover ISBN: 978-1-59540-945-4
eBook ISBN: 978-1-59540-926-3

Cover and Interior Illustrations: Mikaila Maidment

I would like to dedicate this book to:

Theo My ever loving and supporter and believer of my work.

My children Louise, Mark, Anthony and David.
This is their imagination.

My grandparents who gave me my poetic license to write and
do what I know is right.

My beautiful grandchildren:
Asher
Cousteau
Orson
Mark Junior
Kailiana
And to those that follow.

Most of all to all of those that hopefully enjoy the book.

Monty saw a monkey
tickling the lion's toes.

Can you find the worm?

Monty saw a zebra

playing dominoes.

Can you find the worm?

Monty saw a hyena

making chocolate cake.

Can you find the worm?

Monty saw a big brown bear, water skiing on the lake.

Can you find the worm?

Monty saw a
kangaroo trying to
scratch his back.

Can you find the worm?

Monty saw a turtle
running on the track.

Can you find the worm?

Monty saw a rhino
wearing an
evening gown.

Can you find the worm?

Monty saw a hippo

jumping up and down.

Can you find the worm?

Monty saw a python

dancing with the queen.

Can you find the worm?

Monty saw a tiger

eating strawberries

and cream.

Can you find the worm?

Monty saw a panda
wearing sun glasses
looking really cool.

Can you find the worm?

Monty saw a

chimpanzee swimming

in a pool.

Can you find the worm?

Monty saw a penguin

playing with a bee.

Can you find the worm?

Monty saw an elephant

sleeping up a tree.

Can you find the worm?

Monty saw an alligator
wearing a fancy suit.

Can you find the worm?

Monty saw a long
necked giraffe wearing
cowboy boots.

Can you find the worm?

Monty saw a spider

skipping with a snake.

Can you find the worm?

Monty saw a parrot

clearing leaves

with a rake.

Can you find the worm?

Monty saw amazing things while he was at the zoo.

Can you find the worm?

Maybe next time he visits, you can come too.

CPSIA information can be obtained at www.ICGtesting.com
Printed in the USA
BVOW10s1032180315

392212BV00009B/56/P